Gobble Gobble CRASH! BASH

A BARNYARD COUNTING

JULIE STIEGEMEYER
Illustrated by **VALERI GORBACHEV**

Dutton Children's Books

DUTTON CHILDREN'S BOOKS

A division of Penguin Young Readers Group

Published by the Penguin Group

Penguin Group (USA) Inc., 375 Hudson Street, New York, New York 10014, U.S.A.

Penguin Group (Canada), 90 Eglinton Avenue East, Suite 700, Toronto, Ontario, Canada M4P 2Y3 (a division of Pearson Penguin Canada Inc.) • Penguin Books Ltd, 80 Strand, London WC2R 0RL, England • Penguin Ireland, 25 St Stephen's Green, Dublin 2, Ireland (a division of Penguin Books Ltd) • Penguin Group (Australia), 250 Camberwell Road, Camberwell, Victoria 3124, Australia (a division of Pearson Australia Group Pty Ltd) • Penguin Books India Pvt Ltd, 11 Community Centre, Panchsheel Park, New Delhi - 110 017, India Penguin Group (NZ), 67 Apollo Drive, Rosedale, North Shore 0632, New Zealand (a division of Pearson New Zealand Ltd) • Penguin Books (South Africa) (Pty) Ltd, 24 Sturdee Avenue, Rosebank, Johannesburg 2196, South Africa

Penguin Books Ltd, Registered Offices: 80 Strand, London WC2R 0RL, England

Text copyright © 2008 by Julie Stiegemeyer

Illustrations copyright © 2008 by Valeri Gorbachev

All rights reserved.

CIP DATA IS AVAILABLE.

Published in the United States by Dutton Children's Books,

a division of Penguin Young Readers Group

345 Hudson Street, New York, New York 10014

www.penguin.com/youngreaders

Designed by Abby Kuperstock

Manufactured in China

ISBN 978-0-525-47959-8

Special Markets ISBN 978-0-525-42188-7 Not for Resale

This Imagination Library edition is published by Penguin Group (USA), a Pearson company, exclusively for Dolly Parton's Imagination Library, a not-for-profit program designed to inspire a love of reading and learning, sponsored in part by The Dollywood Foundation. Penguin's trade editions of this work are available wherever books are sold.

To Pat Easton and the Peters Township
writing group, who first heard the Gobbles
and nurtured the story through many
revisions. And to Susan Chapek, for help
with the title. Thank you all!

J.S.

For my friend Kim Griswell

V.G.

Fireflies danced in the dark summer sky,
And crickets in the garden played their music in reply.

The farm was very quiet as the night replaced the day,
While **ONE** lonely mare nibbled softly on some hay.

TWO baby cows in the barn fell asleep
To the lullaby of bullfrogs, croaking low and deep.

Settled in the barn with the spiders and a rat,
Were **THREE** fuzzy kittens, cozied close to Mama Cat.

FOUR woolly sheep in a corner of their pen
Lay a-jumbled and a-tumbled in a pile—and then—

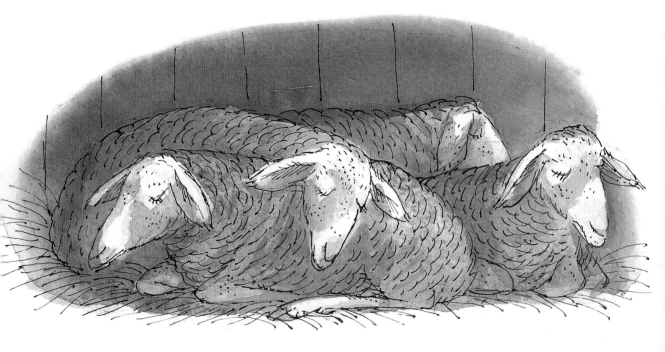

Wow! What a sight! It was strange as strange could be
When flapping wild turkeys flew above the apple tree.

FIVE white geese honked and started laughing hard.
They shook and rolled with laughter in the middle of the yard.

Gobble-Gobble-Crash! Turkeys smashed into the coop
Where the chickens squawked and fluttered—a fluffy feathered group.

Mama Hen grew angry, and she scolded loud and quick,
"Turkeys, can't you calm yourselves? Think of my **SIX** chicks!"

Gobble-Gobble-Crash! Turkeys banged into the house
And scared the living daylights out of Mrs. Maggie Mouse.

"Hey, you naughty turkeys, quit your flying in the night,"
Scolded Mrs. Maggie Mouse, holding **SEVEN** babies tight.

Gobble-Gobble-Crash! Turkeys landed with a thump
In the middle of the barnyard, right beside the water pump.

EIGHT little goats laughed and wrestled in the straw,
And the crows from next door called, *"Caw! Caw! Caw!"*

Gobble-Gobble-Crash! Turkeys found the piggy pen
Where they slopped and made a muddy mess—and then
they flew again.

NINE baby pigs started squealing with delight
'Cause they loved the turkeys flapping in the middle of the night.

Gobble-Gobble-Crash! Turkeys landed near a tree
Where bunny babies danced and sang a happy song: "YIPEE!"

TEN baby robins in their nest yodeled, too—
As the barnyard in the valley had become a noisy zoo.

"What is all that gobbling?" cried the Farmer in his bed.
"Not another turkey mess!" Mrs. Farmer said.

Farmer opened up the window, yelling to the crowd:
"I'm gonna have a turkey feast!" Mr. Farmer vowed.

The animals all gasped when they heard the farmer's scheme.
"We'll save you, turkeys!" came the cry from the barnyard team.
Farmer hurried down the stairs, switching on a light,
Prepared to stop those turkeys from a gobble-crashing flight.

But when . . .

Farmer turned the corner to the barnyard gate,

All the animals were quiet—had he gotten there too late?

He thought he heard some shushes as he stepped beside the coop,

But the turkeys all had vanished—where was that noisy group?

Gobble-Gobble-sshhh!

TEN baby robins slept soundly in their nest,
While **NINE** pink pigs by their mama took a rest.

EIGHT little goats were a-dozin' side by side,
As **SEVEN** tiny mice by their mommy softly sighed.

SIX chicks slept close together in a cage.
Where were the other turkeys? You'll have to turn the page.

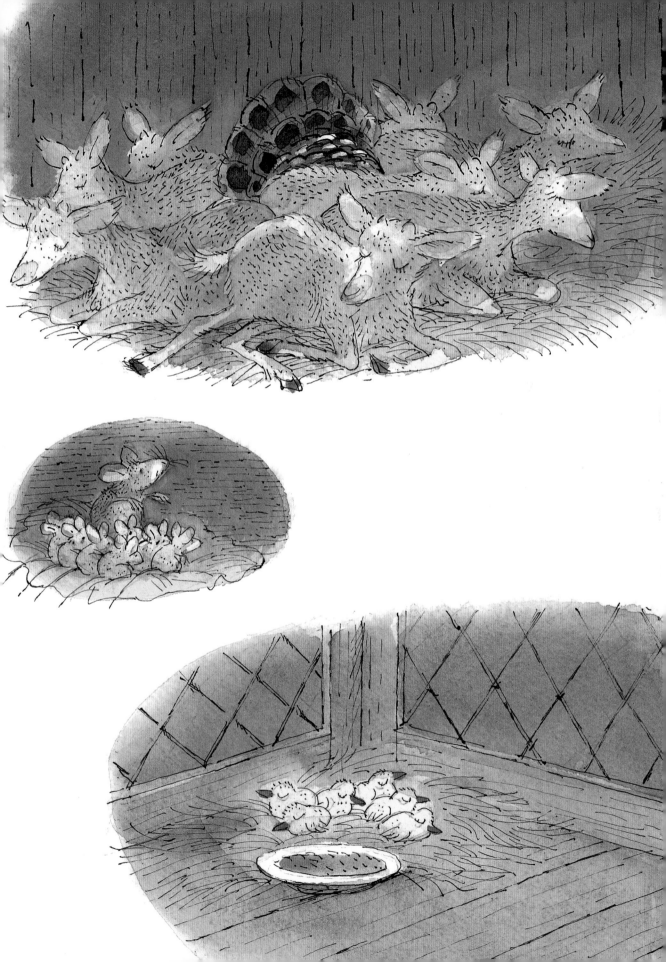

FIVE white geese dozed beside the maple stump,
And **FOUR** woolly sheep hid a feathered turkey rump.

THREE fuzzy kittens and those **TWO** baby cows
Snuggled close to **ONE** horse and some soft and cuddly sows.

Farmer was confused, looked around, and slowly said,
"Well, maybe I was dreaming!"—and he went back up to bed.

But when . . .
Farmer tried to fall asleep, he thought he heard a crash.
A **Gobble-Gobble-Crash!**

Oh no! Another barnyard *bash!*